Title: *King Story*
Author: Howard Pyle

Pyle's *King Story* is **very** poorly written. The literary tale itself, while built on recognizable conventions, falls victim to poor delivery and lack of inspiration. If endeavoring to choose a literary tale, one can find countless other representations that are far more adequate in scope, content and vastly more enjoyable.

In addition, choice illustrations are highly sensual—a characteristic that would be found inappropriate in most classrooms.

KING STORK

For Helen Jones & Betty Johnson
and it wasn't easy!
TSH.

FIRST EDITION

T 04/73

Library of Congress Cataloging in Publication Data

Pyle, Howard.
  King Stork.

  SUMMARY: The King of the Storks grants the drummer
three wishes for carrying him across the river.
  1. Fairy tales. [1. Fairy tales.] I. Hyman,
Trina Schart, illus. II. Title.
PZ8.P99Ki   [Fic]   78-182249
ISBN 0-316-724408

Published simultaneously in Canada
by Little, Brown & Company (Canada) Limited

PRINTED IN THE UNITED STATES OF AMERICA

There was a drummer marching along the high road—forward march!—left, right!—tramp, tramp, tramp!—for the fighting was done, and he was coming home from the wars. By and by he came to a great wide stream of water, and there sat an old man as gnarled and as bent as the hoops in a cooper shop. "Are you going to cross the water?" said he.

"Yes," says the drummer, "I am going to do that if my legs hold out to carry me."

"And will you not help a poor body across?" says the old man.

Now, the drummer was as good-natured a lad as ever stood on two legs. "If the young never gave a lift to the old," says he to himself, "the wide world would not be worth while living in." So he took off his shoes and stockings, and then he bent his back and took the old man on it, and away he started through the water—splash!

But this was no common old man whom the drummer

was carrying, and he was not long finding that out, for the farther he went in the water the heavier grew his load — like work put off until tomorrow — so that, when he was half-way across, his legs shook under him and the sweat stood on his forehead like a string of beads in the shop window. But by and by he reached the other shore, and the old man jumped down from his back.

"Phew!" says the drummer. "I am glad to be here at last!"

And now for the wonder of all this: the old man was an old man no longer, but a splendid tall fellow with hair as yellow as gold. "And who do you think I am?" said he.

But of that the drummer knew no more than the mouse in the haystack, so he shook his head, and said nothing.

"I am king of the storks, and here I have sat for many days; for the wicked one-eyed witch who lives on the glass hill put it upon me for a spell that I should be an old man until somebody should carry me over the water. You are the first to do that, and you shall not lose by it. Here is a little bone whistle; whenever you are in trouble just blow a turn or two on it, and I will be by to help you."

Thereupon King Stork drew a feather cap out of his pocket and clapped it on his head, and away he flew, for he was turned into a great, long, red-legged stork as quick as a wink.

But the drummer trudged on the way he was going, as merry as a cricket, for it is not everybody who cracks his shins against such luck as he had stumbled over, I can tell you. By and by he came to the town over the hill, and there he found great bills stuck up over the walls. They were all of them proclamations. And this is what they said:

The princess of that town was as clever as she was pretty; that was saying a great deal, for she was the handsomest in the whole world. ("Phew! But that is a fine lass for sure and certain," said the drummer.) So it was proclaimed that any lad who could answer a question the princess would ask, and would ask a question the princess could not answer, and would catch the bird that she would be wanting, should have her for his wife and half of the kingdom to boot. ("Hi! But here is luck for a clever lad," says the drummer.) But whoever should fail in any one of the three tasks should have his head chopped off as sure as he lived. ("Ho! But she is a wicked one for all that," says the drummer.)

That was what the proclamation said, and the drummer would have a try for her. "For," said he, "it is a poor fellow who cannot manage a wife when he has her"—and he knew as much about that business as a goose about churning butter. As for chopping off heads, he never bothered his own about that; for, if one never goes out for fear of rain one never catches fish.

Off he went to the king's castle as fast as he could step, and there he knocked on the door, as bold as though his own grandmother lived there.

But when the king heard what the drummer had come for, he took out his pocket-handkerchief and began to wipe his eyes, for he had a soft heart under his jacket, and it made him cry like anything to see another coming to have his head chopped off, as so many had done before him. For there they were, all along the wall in front of the princess's window, like so many apples.

But the drummer was not to be scared away by the king's crying a bit, so in he came, and by and by they all sat down to supper—he and the king and the princess. As for the princess, she was so pretty that the drummer's heart melted inside of him, like a lump of butter on the stove—and that was what she was after. After a while she asked him if he had come to answer a question of hers, and to ask her a question of his, and to catch the bird that she should set him to catch.

"Yes," said the drummer, "I have come to do that very thing." And he spoke as boldly and as loudly as the clerk in church.

"Very well, then," says the princess, as sweet as sugar candy, "just come along tomorrow, and I will ask you your question."

Off went the drummer; he put his whistle to his lips and blew a turn or two, and there stood King Stork, and nobody knows where he stepped from.

"And what do you want?" says he.

The drummer told him everything, and how the princess was going to ask him a question tomorrow morning that he would have to answer, or have his head chopped off.

"Here you have walked into a pretty puddle, and with your eyes open," says King Stork, for he knew that the princess was a wicked enchantress, and loved nothing so much as to get a lad into just such a scrape as the drummer had tumbled into. "But see, here is a little cap and a long feather—the cap is a dark cap, and when you put it on your head one can see you no more than so much thin air. At twelve o'clock at night the princess will come out into the castle garden and will fly away through the air. Then throw your leg over the feather, and it will carry you wherever you want to go; and if the princess flies fast it will carry you as fast and faster."

"Dong! Dong!" The clock struck twelve, and the princess came out of her house; but in the garden was the drummer waiting for her with the dark cap on his head, and he saw her as plain as a pikestaff. She brought a pair of great wings which she fastened to her shoulders, and away she flew. But the drummer was as quick with his tricks as she was with hers; he flung his leg over the feather which King Stork had given him, and away he flew after her, and just as fast as she with her great wings.

By and by they came to a huge castle of shining steel that stood on a mountain of glass. And it was a good thing for the drummer that he had on his cap of darkness, for all around outside of the castle stood fiery dragons and savage lions to keep anybody from going in without leave.

But not a thread of the drummer did they see; in he walked with the princess, and there was a great one-eyed witch with a beard on her chin, and a nose that hooked over her mouth like the beak of a parrot.

"Uff!" said she. "Here is a smell of Christian blood in the house."

"Tut, Mother!" says the princess. "How you talk! Do you not see that there is nobody with me?" For the drummer had taken care that the wind should not blow the cap of darkness off of his head, I can tell you. By and by they sat down to supper, the princess and the witch, but it was little the princess ate, for as fast as anything was put on her plate the drummer helped himself to it, so that it was all gone before she could get a bite.

"Look, Mother!" she said. "I eat nothing, and yet it all goes from my plate; why is that so?" But that the old witch could not tell her, for she could see nothing of the drummer.

"There was a lad came today to answer the question I shall put to him," said the princess. "Now what shall I ask him by way of a question?"

"I have a tooth in the back part of my head," said the witch, "and it has been grumbling a bit; ask him what it is you are thinking about, and let it be that."

Yes; that was a good question for sure and certain, and the princess would give it to the drummer tomorrow, to see what he had to say for himself. As for the drummer, you can guess how he grinned, for he heard every word that they said.

After a while the princess flew away home again, for it was nearly the break of day, and she must be back before the sun rose. And the drummer flew close behind her, but she knew nothing of that.

The next morning up he marched to the king's castle and knocked at the door, and they let him in.

There sat the king and the princess, and lots of folks besides. Well, had he come to answer her question? That was what the princess wanted to know.

Yes; that was the very business he had come about.

Very well, this was the question, and he might have three guesses at it. What was she thinking of at that minute?

Oh, it could be no hard thing to answer such a question as that, for lasses' heads all ran upon the same things more or less. Was it a fine silk dress with glass buttons down the front that she was thinking of now?

No, it was not that.

Then, was it of a good stout lad like himself for a sweetheart, that she was thinking of?

No, it was not that.

No? Then it was the bad tooth that had been grumbling in the head of the one-eyed witch for a day or two past, perhaps.

Dear, dear! But you should have seen the princess's face when she heard this! Up she got and off she packed without a single word, and the king saw without the help of his spectacles that the drummer had guessed right. He was so glad that he jumped up and down and snapped his fingers for joy. Besides that he gave out that bonfires should be lighted all over the town, and that was a fine thing for the little boys.

The next night the princess flew away to the house of the one-eyed witch again, but there was the drummer close behind her just as he had been before.

"Uff!" said the one-eyed witch. "Here is a smell of Christian blood, for sure and certain." But all the same, she saw no more of the drummer than if he had never been born.

"See, Mother," said the princess, "that rogue of a drummer answered my question without winking over it."

"So," said the old witch, "we have missed for once, but the second time hits the mark; he will be asking you a question tomorrow, and here is a book that tells everything that has happened in the world, and if he asks you more than that he is a smart one and no mistake."

After that they sat down to supper again, but it was little the princess ate, for the drummer helped himself out of her plate just as he had done before.

After a while the princess flew away home, and the drummer with her.

"And, now, what will we ask her that she cannot answer?" said the drummer; so off he went back of the house, and blew a turn or two on his whistle, and there stood King Stork.

"And what will we ask the princess," said he, "when she has a book that tells her everything?"

King Stork was not long in telling him that; "Just ask her so and so and so and so," said he, "and she would not dare to answer the question."

Well, the next morning there was the drummer at the castle all in good time; and, had he come to ask her a question? That was what the princess wanted to know.

Oh, yes, he had come for that very thing.

Very well, then, just let him begin, for the princess was ready and waiting, and she wet her thumb, and began to turn over the leaves of her Book of Knowledge.

Oh, it was an easy question the drummer was going to ask, and it needed no big book like that to answer it. The other night he dreamed that he was in a castle all built of shining steel, where there lived a witch with one eye. There was a handsome bit of a lass there who was as great a witch as the old woman herself, but for the life of him he could not tell who she was; now perhaps the princess could make a guess at it.

There the drummer had her as tight as a fly in a bottle, for she did not dare to let folks know that she was a wicked witch like the one-eyed one; so all she could do was to sit there and gnaw her lip. As for the Book of Knowledge, it was no more use to her than a fifth wheel under a cart.

But if the king was glad when the drummer answered the princess's question, he was twice as glad when he found she could not answer his.

All the same, there is more to do yet, and many a slip betwixt the cup and the lip. "The bird I want is the one-eyed raven," said the princess. "Now bring her to me if you want to keep your head off of the wall yonder."

Yes; the drummer thought he might do that as well as another thing. So off he went back of the house to talk to King Stork of the matter.

"Look," said King Stork, and he drew a net out of his pocket as fine as a cobweb and as white as milk. "Take this with you when you go with the princess to the one-eyed witch's house tonight, throw it over the witch's head, and then see what will happen; only when you catch the one-eyed raven you are to wring her neck as soon as you lay hands on her, for if you don't it will be the worse for you."

Well, that night off flew the princess just as she had done before, and off flew the drummer at her heels, until they came to the witch's house, both of them.

"And did you take his head this time?" said the witch.

No, the princess had not done that, for the drummer had asked such and such a question, and she could not answer it; all the same, she had him tight enough now, for she had set it as a task upon him that he should bring her the one-eyed raven, and it was not likely he would be up to doing that. After that the princess and the one-eyed witch sat down to supper together, and the drummer served the princess the same trick that he had done before, so that she got hardly a bite to eat.

"See," said the old witch when the princess was ready to go, "I will go home with you tonight, and see that you get there safe and sound." So she brought out a pair of wings, just like those the princess had, and set them on her shoulders, and away both of them flew with the drummer behind. So they came home without seeing a soul, for the drummer kept his cap of darkness tight upon his head all the while.

"Good night," said the witch to the princess, and "Good night," said the princess to the witch, and the one was for going one way and the other the other. But the drummer had his wits about him sharply enough, and before the old witch could get away he flung the net that King Stork had given him over her head.

"Hi!" But you should have been there to see what happened; for it was a great one-eyed raven, as black as the inside of the chimney, that he had in his net.

Dear, dear, how it flapped its wings and struck with its great beak! But that did no good, for the drummer just wrung its neck, and there was an end of it.

The next morning he wrapped it up in his pocket hand-kerchief and off he started for the king's castle, and there was the princess waiting for him, looking as cool as butter in the well, for she felt sure the drummer was caught in the trap this time.

"And have you brought the one-eyed raven with you?" she said.

"Oh, yes," said the drummer, and here it was wrapped up in this handkerchief.

But when the princess saw the raven with its neck wrung, she gave a great shriek and fell to the floor. There she lay and they had to pick her up and carry her out of the room.

But everybody saw that the drummer had brought the bird she had asked for, and all were as glad as glad could be. The king gave orders that they should fire off the town cannon, just as they did on his birthday, and all the little boys out in the street flung up their hats and caps and cried, "Hurrah! Hurrah!"

But the drummer went off back of the house. He blew a turn or two on his whistle, and there stood King Stork. "Here is your dark cap and your feather," says he, "and it is I who am thankful to you, for they have won me a real princess for a wife."

"Yes, good," says King Stork. "You have won her, sure enough, but the next thing is to keep her; for a lass is not cured of being a witch as quickly as you seem to think, and after one has found one's eggs one must roast them and butter them into the bargain. See now, the princess is just as wicked as ever she was before, and if you do not keep your eyes open she will trip you up after all. So listen to what I tell you. Just after you are married, get a great bowl of fresh milk and a good, stiff switch. Pour the milk over the princess when you are alone together, and after that hold tight to her and lay on the switch, no matter what happens, for that is the only way to save yourself and to save her."

Well, the drummer promised to do as King Stork told him, and by and by came the wedding day. Off he went over to the dairy and got a fresh pan of milk, and out he went into the woods and cut a stout hazel switch, as thick as his finger.

As soon as he and the princess were alone together he emptied the milk all over her; then he caught hold of her and began laying on the switch for dear life.

It was well for him that he was a brave fellow and had been to the wars, for, instead of the princess, he held a great black cat that glared at him with her fiery eyes, and growled and spat like anything. But that did no good, for the drummer just shut his eyes and laid on the switch harder than ever.

Then—puff!—instead of a black cat it was like a great, savage wolf, that snarled and snapped at the drummer with its red jaws; but the drummer just held fast and made the switch fly, and the wolf scared him no more than the black cat had done.

So out it went, like a light of a candle, and there was a great snake that lashed its tail and shot out its forked tongue and spat fire. But no; the drummer was no more frightened at that than he had been at the wolf and the cat, and, dear, dear! how he dressed the snake with his hazel switch.

Last of all, there stood the princess herself. "Oh, dear husband!" she cried. "Let me go, and I will promise to be good all the days of my life."

"Very well," says the drummer, "and that is the tune I like to hear."

That was the way he gained the best of her, whether it was the bowl of milk or the hazel switch, for afterwards she was as good a wife as ever churned butter; but what did it is a question that you will have to answer for yourself. All the same, she tried no more of her tricks with him, I can tell you. And so this story comes to an end, like everything else in the world.

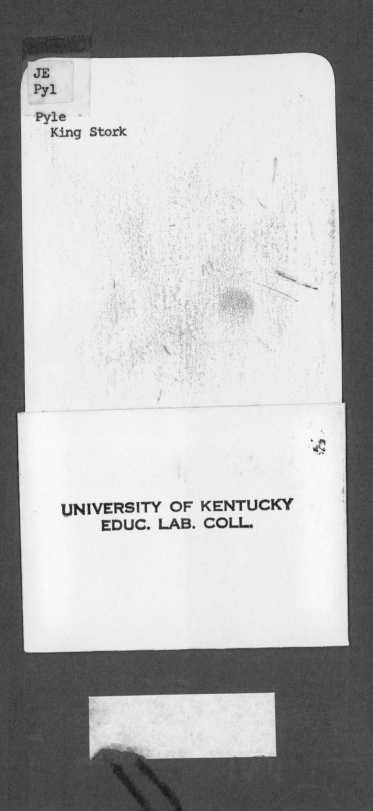